Here Comes
TEACHER
CAT

Here Comes
TEACHER

CAT

by
DEBORAH UNDERWOOD

pictures by
CLAUDIA RUEDA

Dial Books for Young Readers

Psst—Cat!

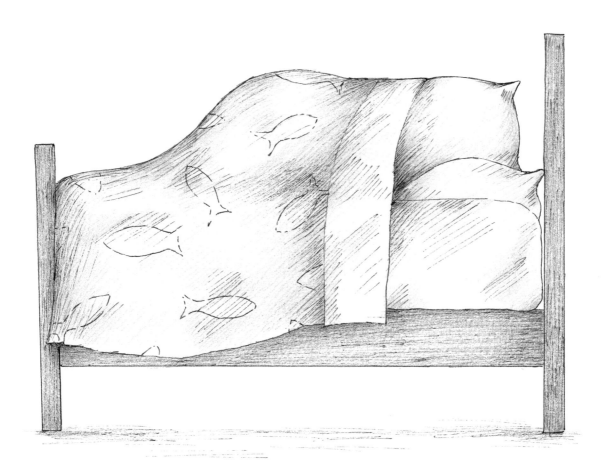

I know you're napping,
but this is an emergency!

Ms. Melba had to go to the doctor!

She needs you to teach Kitty School today.

Dog is on vacation.

And I suspect Santa Claus, the Easter Bunny, and the Tooth Fairy aren't available either.

Yes. There will be kittens there.

That's kind of the idea of
Kitty School.

Where are you going?!

Come on—kittens can be fun!

Oh, Cat. Ms. Melba has always helped YOU out.

Remember how she made you that nice catnip pillow?

And brought you soup when you were sick?

Way to go, Cat!

It's only for a few hours.

Goodness, you look surprisingly
happy to be here.

Wait a minute . . . Cat? Cat!
Where are you?

Nice try, Cat.

It's not nap time yet.

Okay, Cat—what are you
going to do first?

Music? That's a great idea!

Hey! Where are you going?

Um . . .

Cat? . . . CAT?

That might be too loud
for the . . .

...class next door.

Maybe something else?

Building time?

That sounds fun!

Cat, what on earth is
all of that?

You're building a . . . what?

A fountain that spouts fish??

I think the kitty wants
to help you!

Wow! It works!

I guess that takes care of
snack time too!

Art is next? Great!

Aw, Cat! The kitty has
a paint set for you!

Cat?

Uh—what are you doing?

Cat, do you think that's
a good idea?

Oh dear.

Oh no!

I think I hear
Ms. Melba!

What are you
going to do?

Good thinking,
kitty!

Hurry!

Welcome back, Ms. Melba!

Oh dear, Cat.

I guess you'd better tell her.

Wait—where are the kitties going?

Yes!

They played music, and built things,
and had some fish, and painted!

Hey! *And* they learned to
talk with signs!

Just like you, Cat!

And it looks like *you* might have learned something about kitties.

Cat, is it time to say good-bye?

Cat?

Aw. Looks like it's finally nap time.

Sweet dreams, Cat!

For teachers everywhere, with thanks —D.U.
For I.E., my art history teacher —C.R.

Dial Books for Young Readers
Penguin Young Readers Group
An imprint of Penguin Random House LLC
375 Hudson Street
New York, New York 10014

ISBN 9780399539053

Manufactured in China on acid-free paper

10 9 8 7 6 5 4 3 2 1

Design by Jennifer Kelly
Text set in Handwriter OT

THE ART WAS MADE WITH INK AND COLOR PENCILS ON WHITE PAPER, SURROUNDED BY HUNDREDS OF CATS (INK CATS!).